D1094650

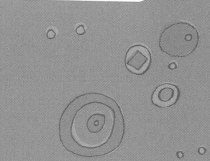

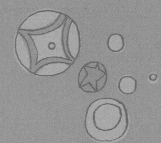

To Ailsa

First published 2010 by Macmillan Children's Books
a division of Macmillan Publishers Limited
20 New Wharf Road, London N1 9RR
Basingstoke and Oxford
Associated companies throughout the world
www.panmacmillan.com

ISBN: 978-0-230-71218-8

A CIP catalogue record for this book is available from the British Library.

Printed in Italy

natalie russell

brown rabbit

in the city

MACMILLAN CHILDREN'S BOOKS

Brown Rabbit stood waiting beside the bus stop at the park. He was going to the city to see his friend and he was very excited.

Brown Rabbit had never been to the city before.

He listened quietly to the birds and smiled as the cool breeze tickled his ears.

It will be nice to see Little Rabbit, he thought.

When the bus arrived, Brown Rabbit hopped
on board and went upstairs for the best view.
Then he counted the stops, until . . .

. . . there she was, waiting for him,
right where she said she would be.

"These are for you," said Brown Rabbit, and Little Rabbit smiled.

Then Little Rabbit took Brown Rabbit to her favourite cafe.

She was so excited — there was so much she wanted
him to see. Before Brown Rabbit could finish his cake,
Little Rabbit said, "Let's go, there's not much time!"
and she whisked him away.

Up a tall building,
(Smile at the camera!)

Down a crowded street,
(Watch your step!)

MUSEUM

LIBRARY

THEATRE

PRETZEL

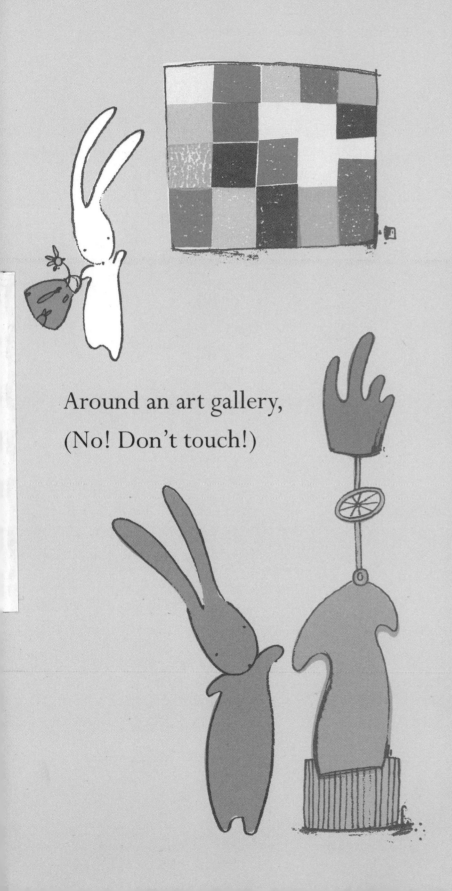

Around an art gallery,
(No! Don't touch!)

And underground to catch a train.
(Here it comes!)

57 TH

Everything in the city
moved so fast . . .

. . . including Little Rabbit!

They went across busy roads,

and in and out of many shops.

Hats, bags, bangles and scarves.
Little Rabbit wanted to try them all.

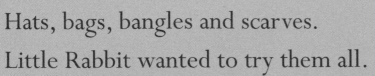

perfume

Brown Rabbit stopped to catch his
breath and brush the dust from his ears.
"Keep up!" called Little Rabbit.

Then Brown Rabbit saw a beautiful guitar. It made him think of his old guitar, which he'd once played for Little Rabbit while she danced in the park.

He turned to Little Rabbit. He wanted her to see.

But she was busy buying
Brown Rabbit a big bow tie.

"Just perfect for the party,"
she said.

Brown Rabbit sighed. He was
too tired for a party.

At the party, Brown Rabbit watched as
Little Rabbit danced. He couldn't join in;
his feet were too sore from all the rushing around.

So Brown Rabbit sat by himself
and waited . . .

and waited.

After a while, when Little
Rabbit went to find him . . .

Brown Rabbit had gone.

Little Rabbit searched the room.

She searched the street.

She looked everywhere.

But it was no use.

Why did Brown Rabbit leave, she wondered.

Then she thought about how busy they had been – and suddenly she knew what was wrong. "I hardly spoke to him all day," she sighed. "I said there was no time, and now I've upset my best friend."

Feeling sad, Little Rabbit walked slowly home.

But as she passed her favourite cafe, she saw something that made her stop.

It was Brown Rabbit! He was sitting in the cafe eating a slice of carrot cake.

Little Rabbit rushed inside.

"I'm sorry!" she sniffed. "I just wanted you to see the city."

Brown Rabbit stood up and wiped away her tears.

"But I came to see you, not the city," he replied, and Little Rabbit smiled.

The next afternoon the two rabbits
strolled slowly through the city.

"I have a surprise for you," said
Little Rabbit, and she led him down
a quiet street, through an old gate
and into a beautiful garden.

It's just like home, thought Brown Rabbit.

And there on a bench was a present from
Little Rabbit. It was perfect.

As the sun set over the the city, Brown Rabbit
played his new guitar and Little Rabbit danced.

Brown Rabbit's bus came
and went. But Brown Rabbit
didn't mind.

After all, they had all the time
in the world.

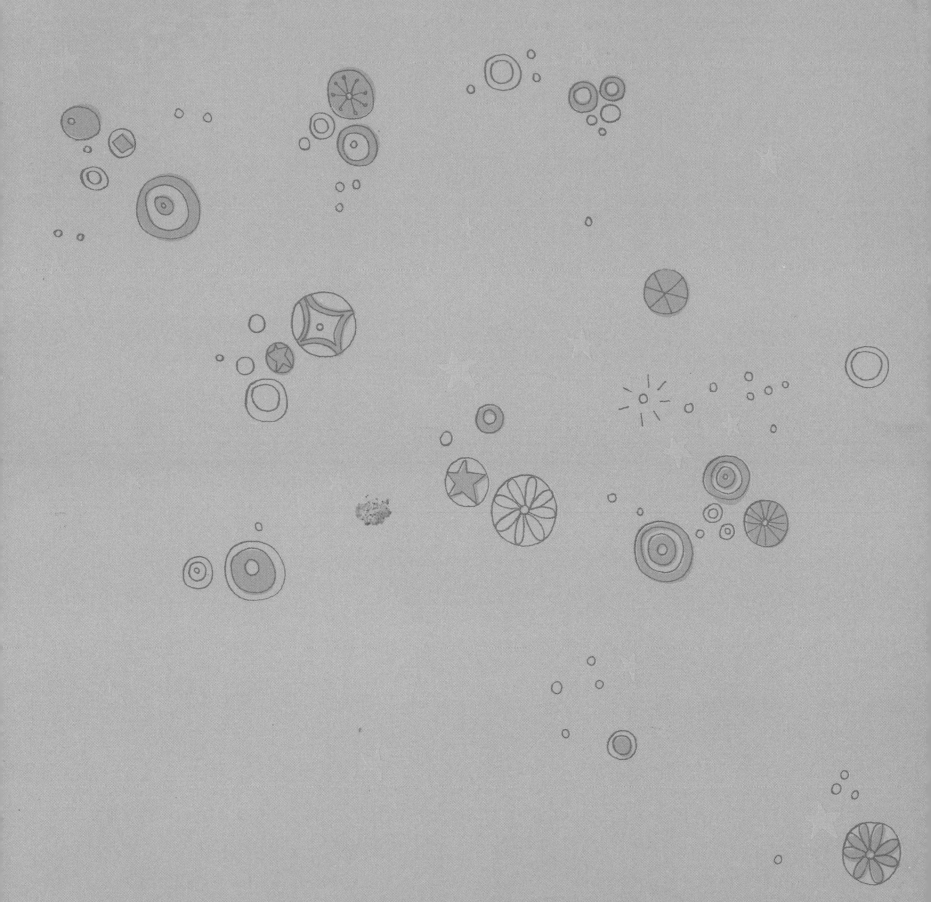